The Game

by Bekah Brunstetter

‖ SAMUEL FRENCH ‖

FOR PRODUCTION INQUIRIES

UNITED STATES AND CANADA
info@concordtheatricals.com
1-866-979-0447

UNITED KINGDOM AND EUROPE
licensing@concordtheatricals.co.uk
020-7054-7298

Each title is subject to availability from Concord Theatricals Corp., depending upon country of performance. Please be aware that *THE GAME* may not be licensed by Concord Theatricals Corp. in your territory. Professional and amateur producers should contact the nearest Concord Theatricals Corp. office or licensing partner to verify availability.

No one shall make any changes in this title(s) for the purpose of production. No part of this book may be reproduced, stored in a retrieval system, scanned, uploaded, or transmitted in any form, by any means, now known or yet to be invented, including mechanical, electronic, digital, photocopying, recording, videotaping, or otherwise, without the prior written permission of the publisher. No one shall share this title(s), or any part of this title(s), through any social media or file hosting websites.

For all inquiries regarding motion picture, television, online/digital and other media rights, please contact Concord Theatricals Corp.

MUSIC AND THIRD-PARTY MATERIALS USE NOTE

Licensees are solely responsible for obtaining formal written permission from copyright owners to use copyrighted music and/or other copyrighted third-party materials (e.g. artworks, logos) in the performance of this play and are strongly cautioned to do so. If no such permission is obtained by the licensee, then the licensee must use only original music and materials that the licensee owns and controls. Licensees are solely responsible and liable for clearances of all third-party copyrighted materials, including without limitation music, and shall indemnify the copyright owners of the play(s) and their licensing agent, Concord Theatricals Corp., against any costs, expenses, losses and liabilities arising from the use of such copyrighted third-party materials by licensees. For music, please contact the appropriate music licensing authority in your territory for the rights to any incidental music.

IMPORTANT BILLING AND CREDIT REQUIREMENTS

If you have obtained performance rights to this title, please refer to your licensing agreement for important billing and credit requirements.

THE GAME was commissioned and produced by Playmakers Repertory in Chapel Hill, North Carolina in April 2024. The performance was directed by Vivienne Benesch, with sets by Lee Savage, costumes by Pamela A. Bond, lighting design by Carolina Ortiz Herrera, and sound design by Kate Marvin. The Production Stage Manager was Sarah Smiley. The cast was as follows:

ALYSSA . . . . .Megan Ketch

HOMER . . . . Lucas Dixon

JEN . . . . .Sanjana Taskar

CLEO . . . . Elizabeth Dye

RHONDA . . . . Kathryn Hunter-Williams

MYRA . . . . Cinny Strickland

CHARACTERS

ALYSSA – (30s/40s) a high-functioning multitasking Woman with squishy insides; our leader.

HOMER – (30s/40s) her husband, a Man in a basement entrenched in a virtual world.

JEN – (30s/40s) a very good photographer, a terrible socializer.

CLEO – (20s) a pregnant military wife, and this is her entire personality.

RHONDA – (40s/50s) a serial online shopper, image obsessed.

MYRA – (70s/80s) a gentle but quietly brilliant little old lady.

Note on casting: Jen and Rhonda should be played by women of color.

SETTING

A mid-sized town near a military base.

TIME

Now.

AUTHOR'S NOTES

Note on performance: Do your best with the overlapping dialogue, move things around as you find a natural rhythm of women anxiously talking over each other.

Note on time: This play takes place in the year your production is produced. You may adjust any years mentioned to be relative to the year you are producing this play.

Prologue

(The sounds of war. Epic, all-out, timeless war. All of the wars throughout time.)

(Horns and shouts, broken limbs. Cries and radio crackles, planes going down, sons lost, mothers crying by phones, arrows ricocheting off shields. Bombs falling.)

(Then, the sounds get sucked into a Game, and fade away.)

(All that's left is **ALYSSA**. *She has a baby strapped to her chest, its face turned into her breasts. She moves towards us, epic music swelling,[*] like she's about to welcome us to another world, like she's about to tell us that her parents were Wolves, or how she once climbed up a Waterfall –)*

ALYSSA. Welcome to THE GAMEEEEE!

*(***ALYSSA** *then becomes herself. A regular human woman with a mental To-Do list longer than her own life.)*

Okay, first and foremost, I can't be fully objective here, because, the thing is, *I do not play Games.* I just find them to be a complete waste of time. Even as a

---

[*] A license to produce *The Game* does not include a performance license for any third-party or copyrighted music. Licensees should create an original composition or use music in the public domain. For further information, please see the Music and Third-Party Materials Use Note on page iii.

kid, I remember *Mall Madness* feeling like a time suck, and *Candy Land*, when you're done, you have to put all of the pieces back into the box and it's just *so many pieces*, and I was always very distracted by that.

Don't get me wrong! I'm fun. I just think work is fun!

I'm an architect, I specialize in sustainable retail spaces.

> *(Her phone dings with a text.)*

Actually let me just –

> *(She stops and reads the full text. It fills her with a microdose of rage, but she compartmentalizes hard, she's a chest of fucking drawers. She starts to respond quickly to the text.)*

> *(As she texts:)*

Sorry.

But I'm not all work and no play. I like to exercise! And - organize drawers.

And – that's it.

> *(She's done with her text manifesto. Gives us her full attention.)*

But my husband, he *loves* Games. *Video* Games. They're his go-to. His resting state. Which is fine. They make him happy. And I want him to be happy. But lately – it's become something more. It's not a break from life, it *is* life.

What you're about to see is *not* a simulation, or hyperbole. It's not a marketing strategy and it's not a cry for help. Even though actually – it might be that.

I present to you an ACTUAL image of my husband, playing The Game. And yes, this is to scale.

*(Her husband **HOMER** appears, playing The Game.)*

(He's at home, tucked into his favorite chair which seems to have formed around him.)

(He wears a headset and holds an Xbox controller.)

(He's completely consumed by The Game.)

(There's a box of cheese crackers next to him.)

*(The Game's colors and shapes move across **ALYSSA**'s face. To her, they're primitive, childish. She doesn't understand them.)*

*(But still, **ALYSSA** looks at him with so, so much love. And a bit of pity, too.)*

HOMER. Yeah, man. I see him. What's with this noob?!

(Then.)

No no no GO GO GO – I can't see – I'm in the fog.

Nah, I can't respawn. My health's bad.

(Then.)

Oh SHIT! There's a mob up there! Let's rush these fools!

ALYSSA. *(To us.)* He has a Master's degree in biochemical engineering.

HOMER.

YEEEEEE-AH! DUAL WIELD, BABY!	
	ALYSSA.
Wait, watch the side, watch the side –	What's that saying? Behind every successful man is a woman.

HOMER.

(Like someone died.)

NOOOOOOOO
OOOOO!!!!!!!!!!
WHAT?!!! WHAT WAS
THAT?!

Are you griefing me,
dude?! Bad manners.

Okay, then go back in.
Around the *side*.
WHAT? NO!

You can't pee right now,
man! I've had to pee since
we dropped in, HOLD
YOUR PEE!

ALYSSA.

Behind every *un*successful
woman, is a man.

Here's mine: Behind every
Successful *Woman* is a
Man, playing a video game.

ALYSSA. Okay, so. *"The Game"* – which is the actual name of The Game – like did everyone at the game-making company just give up? – It's a massively successful Multiplayer Online Roleplaying Game, or MORPG, an acronym that I learned deep in a Reddit thread about Gaming addiction.

He plays *all* day. Every day. Seven days a week.

HOMER. DUDDDDDEEEEEEEEEE!

> *(He laughs, joyously. Then shoves some crackers into his mouth.)*

> (**ALYSSA** *watches him, a bit sadly.*)

ALYSSA. I don't fully understand The Game, but from what I've gathered, the basic premise is that the world has been at least partially destroyed by nuclear war, or climate change, or Facebook? And all that's left are dirty sports bras, and burnt down buildings, and weapons. Lots of weapons. And a single traffic cone. There doesn't appear to be any coffee anywhere, that's what REALLY stresses me out. It's up to the Players to band together, fight the Enemy, and survive. I don't understand who the Enemy is, but sometimes, they're in a sports bra, too.

I don't get it. And I want to. *I want to get it.*

(Then.)

Out of fairness, maybe I should let *him* explain it.

(She turns to him.)

Hey, honey?

(He keeps playing.)

Homer.

(No response.)

HOMER.

(He pops a single ear out of a headset. He's warm with her, but distracted.)

Yeah, baby!

ALYSSA. Do you have a minute?

HOMER. I'm playing – lemmee just get to a / checkpoint –

No no no no –

ALYSSA. Can you pause it?

HOMER. No, I can't –

(He gets killed.)

GAHHHHHHHHHHHH

ALYSSA. What?

HOMER. I died.

ALYSSA. ...It's okay, though. You're still a living man!

HOMER. I know! But I was playing. Now I have to start over.

Sorry, did you need something?

ALYSSA. I was wondering if you could explain The Game to me?

HOMER. Really? You want me to?

ALYSSA. Yeah! I wanna hear about it!

*(**HOMER** has been waiting for what feels like his whole life for her to take interest in The Game.)*

*(**HOMER** takes a breath, then:)*

HOMER. Okay, so. The year is 2264, the planet is fried, water and resources are scarce. It's an open world.

ALYSSA. Open! / Right!

HOMER. You can go anywhere. There's a lot to explore. You can go solo, or can play with a Clan. There's sidequests, but your main goal is to get to the great Ancient City, it's been abandoned since the twelfth century B.C.E. but now it's the only inhabitable place on Earth.

ALYSSA. And it's in – / America?

HOMER. It's where survivors have started a new civilization. It can take forever to get there, depending on your XP –

ALYSSA. *(She knows this.)* XP! Experience points!

HOMER. Yep, you gain experience points as you gain new skills, skills accumulate with the levels based on your output. So you start in the blue zone, that's where the bulk of your resources are, clean water, fuel, crickets –

ALYSSA. Crickets?

HOMER. Main source of food. That's the future.

ALYSSA. *(To us.)* Am I the only one who doesn't want to eat crickets?

HOMER. Then you get to purple, it's a good place to just grind and earn some cash.

If you make it to the Ancient City, that's where you fight the Big Boss –

(**ALYSSA** *is now replying to an email on her phone.*)

Are you listening?

ALYSSA. Yes! *Yes*. Sorry – it's Carly, she's completely incompetent.

HOMER. It's like nine o'clock at night. Thought you were gonna / start setting some boundaries.

ALYSSA. I know. I just need to get this one thing out –

HOMER. *(On headset.)* MARCIO! 'Sup. No, I'm still here. I was just on mute!

ALYSSA. Who's Marcio?

HOMER. He's a guy I play with. I've told you about him. He's only avail Wednesday and Friday nights because of his class schedule.

ALYSSA. His class schedule?

HOMER. He goes to State.

ALYSSA. *(To us.)* A thirty-nine-year-old man! Playing a game, with a college kid!

(**HOMER** *gets sucked back into The Game.*)

HOMER. *(Into headset.)* Yeah, I'm here!

(**ALYSSA** *faces us again.*)

ALYSSA. He didn't used to be like this.

ALYSSA. He used to be a God. Or, he was mine. We were partners.

> *(She feels like she said too much, so she stops.)*
>
> *(She watches him play, sadly.)*
>
> *(Faces us, again.)*

A marriage is a treaty. You both agree to be happy. Because when one of you isn't, it's contagious. When they're sad, you miss them.

(To **HOMER.***)* I miss you. I miss our peaceful world.

> *(A moment.)*
>
> *(Back to us.)*

A marriage is an entire world.

So this –

> *(She points to her* **HUSBAND,** *playing The Game.)*

This means *War*. And in times of war, we must make sacrifices, we must be brave, I must step outside my comfort zone.

> *(She steels herself.)*

What I'm about to do is not safe. It's dangerous and inadvisable, but it's the byproduct of *months* of desperation.

> *(She can't believe she's about to say this.)*

I'm going to invite a bunch of random Women that I met on the internet into my House.

On a weeknight.

> *(Ding-dong!)*

Greek Yogurt

(We're now in Alyssa's living room.)

(She's set out snacks.)

*(She's surrounded by **WOMEN** that she's never met before today.)*

*(**CLEO**, twenties, is visibly four or five months pregnant, wide-eyed and young.)*

*(**MYRA** is in her seventies and doesn't quite seem to understand exactly where she is, but she's up for anything.)*

*(**RHONDA** is in her late forties and wears ridiculous clothes that you might find deeeeep in a clearance rack, like a sweater with a sparkly parrot on it. She looks like she's trying to be eight different women at once.)*

*(**JEN**, thirties, is quiet, terrifyingly smart, and a bit awkward. She's hidden behind her camera, a really nice Canon. Every now and then, she snaps a picture of someone.)*

(They all buzz with nervous energy, balance little plates on their laps, all desperately wanting to be liked, to fit in.)

(It's all fake yet earnest, and completely terrifying.)

ALYSSA.	**RHONDA.** *(To **JEN**.)*
I have some Dip!	Great jacket, where's it from?

CLEO.

Yay this is fun!

MYRA.

I'm VERY sensitive to sugar!
But I eat it anyways!

JEN.

I found it at an
airport? I think?

RHONDA.

It looks like Zara, is it
Zara?

ALYSSA.

Yeah, I can't do
sugar anymore.
Just wine!

JEN.

No clue!

MYRA.

My mother had mai tais
for breakfast when she was
pregnant with me. And I
turned out mostly fine!

RHONDA.

I could get you fifty
bucks for that on
Poshmark.

JEN.

Posh what now?

CLEO.

Better safe than sorry!
*(To **ALYSSA**.)*
Are you breastfeeding?

RHONDA.

It's an app where you
can sell your clothes.
I am HOOKED!

JEN.

Oh, no thanks. I'm –
wearing it.

ALYSSA. *(To **JEN**.)*

What were you saying, about
melatonin?
*(To **CLEO**.)*
Oh, God no.
*(To **ALL**.)*
Would anyone like some dip?

RHONDA.

Oooh, it looks yummy!

CLEO.

I'm just going to put a little bit on my plate or I'll eat it *all*. Mmm.

What's in this?

ALYSSA.

Greek yogurt.

MYRA.

The other day – I had something called *Kale* Slaw!

JEN.

Coleslaw! I get it!

MYRA.

KALE slaw!

RHONDA. *(Of dip.)*

Are you sure this is Greek yogurt?

ALYSSA.

Yep!

JEN. *(To* **ALYSSA***.)*

Oh, it helps me sleep, I'll take like, eight melatonin. It's non-habit-forming!

ALYSSA.

I have the hardest time falling asleep. Can't turn off my brain!

MYRA.

Menopause!

CLEO.

Sorry, I have to stretch.

(She gets up to do it.)

RHONDA.

Girl, can I tell you, you got a cute little body. You better kiss that body goodbye, though.

*(***JEN*** *snaps a picture.)*

JEN. *(To* **MYRA***.)* Sorry. Do you mind?

MYRA. Not at all. What a beautiful camera.

JEN. Thanks! It's my baby.

MYRA. Do you have any – human babies?

JEN. I do not!

MYRA. That's alright! We're still women!

(To **ALYSSA**.) This dip is so nice! Is it mayonnaise?

CLEO. I'm excited! For the baby.

ALYSSA. **IT'S GREEK YOGURT.**

(Everyone is now quiet, all eyes on her.)

ALYSSA. Okay! I guess I'll start! Hello, women of Troy! I think this is everyone who RSVP'd. I know this probably could've been a Zoom, but I find in-person meetings to be so much more productive. So here you all are. In my living room!

(She laughs anxiously, then:)

Thank you all so much for coming and for responding to my post. We're here because we share a common goal. We've all lost Partners to The Game. So I really want us to just, ah. Be here for each other, with our, ah. Feelings, and – wine and – music – Alexa, play me some hype music!

(Music in a genre you like starts playing, too loud.*)

(**CLEO** bops to it.)

MYRA. (Reminding her.) Is the baby sleeping?

---

* A license to produce The Game does not include a performance license for any third-party or copyrighted music. Licensees should create an original composition or use music in the public domain. For further information, please see the Music and Third-Party Materials Use Note on page iii.

ALYSSA. Right. I have a baby!

ALEXA, QUIETER!

*(The music softens. **ALYSSA** puts a hand on the baby's sleeping butt.)*

CLEO. What's his name?

ALYSSA. Hmm?

CLEO. Your baby.

ALYSSA. Oh! Phillip, I think. We should introduce ourselves. I'll go first. As you know, I'm Alyssa.

(They all mumble polite "Hi, Alyssa"s.)

My husband, Homer, suffers from what I would call a mild to moderate case of internet gaming addiction.

Oh, before I forget, if he comes upstairs, just pretend this is a book club.

RHONDA. He's *here*?

ALYSSA. He's downstairs. But he usually stays down there.

RHONDA. What book did we read?

CLEO. Quick! Someone say a book!!!

JEN. *War and Peace*!

ALYSSA. Yes! Or, *Eat, Pray, Love*. Can we all agree on *Eat, Pray, Love*?

(Everyone murmurs their agreement.)

(Her phone dings with a work text.)

Sorry –

(While she fires off a response:) So to kick us off, I threw together a little presentation.

(A giant projection screen appears in the room, perhaps zips down from the ceiling, with an immaculate PowerPoint presentation on it.)

*(**RHONDA** puts on a ridiculous, giant pair of fashion glasses, like how is her face even able to support them?)*

RHONDA. *(Proud.)* Poshmark! Twenty bucks.

(Confessing.) They do not help me see.

*(**ALYSSA** clicks through the presentation like we're at her TED Talk.)*

ALYSSA. What I've got here are real data points. These are the actual hours my husband has spent in the last month playing The Game. You'll see that the hours spent on The Game negatively affect our gross income –

*(**ALYSSA** clicks to a new slide.)*

And here, you'll find my assessment, which is that basically, at this rate of Game consumption, he'll be dead by Spring of next year, and I'll be in prison, for murdering him.

MYRA. Oh, dear.

ALYSSA. Oh, and there's a handout!

*(**ALYSSA** goes for a stack of carefully assembled and stapled paper packets. She hands it to **RHONDA**.)*

Can you pass these down, please?

(The packets are dispersed.)

So this is just a quick list I threw together of some common video game terminology. We can quiz each other. Someone try me. Anyone! Shout one of them out!

MYRA. *(Reading off sheet.)* Spawn Camping!

ALYSSA. To Spawn Camp! To hover around an area where people respawn, and immediately kill them.

RHONDA. My husband Spawn Camps!

ALYSSA. Sorry, did you want to introduce yourself?

(All eyes are now on her.)

RHONDA. I'm Rhonda. My husband's addicted to The Game. Like, bad. It's like I've got a third teenager. Except for the fact that my actual children don't even play it. They're in their rooms watching YouTube YouTube.

MYRA. What is – what did you say?

JEN. It's YouTube videos about YouTube videos.

(RHONDA*'s phone dings.)*

RHONDA. Ooh! I just sold your blazer on Poshmark for forty bucks!

JEN. But I'm wearing it –

RHONDA. We'll talk later.

MYRA. Poshmark? I think that's what my great-grandmother died of.

RHONDA. No, It's an online re-sale marketplace. I have Ambassador status.

I have luxury items, preteen clothes, and a *lot* of gently worn athleisure. I'm a bit of a clothes whore.

CLEO. Isn't it clothes – horse?

RHONDA. No, I think it's whore.

ALYSSA. *(Back on track.)* My husband – Homer – he says he's playing with friends, but he's never met these people in real life, so ARE they his friends?!

MYRA. I was hoping *we* / could all be friends.

JEN. *(Of graph.)* If it makes you feel any better, Hannah plays like twice as much as your husband.

ALYSSA. And Hannah is your –?

JEN. My partner.

MYRA. *(Proud to know.)* I think she means her *sexual* partner.

JEN. Thank you.

> *(It's awkward, so.)*

Now's a great time to say hi, I'm Jen. And – yeah.

> *(**CLEO** raises her hand.)*

ALYSSA. Yes! Question?

CLEO. Hi, I'm pregnant! I mean, I'm Cleo! My husband is Private First Class Brad Hubert. We just moved here a few months ago. We're due in November. This is really nice! To be around other girls.

(Correcting herself.) Women! I'm a woman.

RHONDA. *(Of her stomach.)* Honey, I would say you are.

CLEO. So wait, girls play The Game too?

JEN. Yeah, it's not really typically a quote unquote "male" space anymore –

ALYSSA. *(Consulting her research.)* Forty-five percent of gamers are women.

CLEO. *(Worried.)* Like – *pretty* girls?

RHONDA. It doesn't matter. They can't actually see each other. That's another thingie, called Twat.

ALYSSA. It's called *Twitch*. Twitch is the online gaming *streaming* platform, where people can watch each other play video games. It's on page four of the handout.

CLEO. Why would you want to watch someone else play a video game?

ALYSSA. *THANK* YOU. EXACTLY. I DON'T KNOW.

Oh, does anyone want a mini scone? They're from the drug store.

MYRA. Oh! Thank / you!

JEN. Don't mind if I do.

ALYSSA. Tell me if they're good. Oh, I haven't had bread since 2017.

MYRA. Delicious!

(**ALYSSA** *offers a mini scone to* **CLEO**.)

CLEO. Oh, no thank you. I shouldn't!

RHONDA. Girl, if anyone should be eating drugstore mini scones it's you. You're growing a whole other person!

CLEO. But the "eating for two" thing is actually a myth. And Brad likes me little.

RHONDA. "Little"?

ALYSSA. ...But you're pregnant.

MYRA. Does anyone need any good crockpot recipes?

Really, all a woman needs is a crockpot!

ALYSSA. Oh, I actually hate to cook.

RHONDA. Have you tried Orange Spatula?! They send you *everything*. Even the forks!

CLEO. Is it like Blue Apron?

RHONDA. Kinda, but it's already made. You just heat it up.

JEN. So it's takeout?

ALYSSA. I don't want to do Blue Spatula Apron. Let's bring our focus back to some strategies –

MYRA. *(To* **ALYSSA**.*)* Really, with all of the time you spent making these charts and handouts, you could've put a chicken in the crockpot.

ALYSSA. Thank you, Myra? Is it Myra?

MYRA. Yes!

ALYSSA. Did you want to introduce yourself?

MYRA. Oh! Yes. Hello. I'm Myra. My husband, Mark! He managed the Carpet Warehouse, over on Reynolds, but he's since retired. I just thought it'd be nice – to make some new friends! It's hard to make new friends, at my age. I asked my dentist if she'd like to go for a walk around the lake! But she hasn't responded to my message. It was on Facebook. But there's three of me on there, for some reason. So maybe I sent it from the wrong one. One time I sent a message – to myself.

(Contemplating this.) I didn't answer it.

(They're all still just looking at her.)

But yes! Mark, he – plays – The Game! So much – shooting! And killing!

(Tries a gun sound.) Pew pew pew!

ALYSSA. How, HOW can this constant immersion in such a violent space be good for them?!

RHONDA. Oh, well, apparently it's not JUST the violence from the video games that create a violent person. The person has to also be schizophrenic, or lonely, or have gone to public school.

JEN. I went to / public school. I loved it!

CLEO. I think Brad might just be bored. It's always like this when he gets back from a training. He doesn't know what to do with himself. And I feel so helpless.

(Then.)

But it's what I signed up for!

(*Then, suddenly.*)

God Bless America!

ALYSSA. Homer's not happy either. I can feel it. It has a smell. I can't get it out of my clothes. It's in our sheets. Ever since he got fired –

(*She realizes she's said too much.*)

Sorry. That's his business. I shouldn't.

(*They all murmur their sympathy, fill the silence for her.*)

RHONDA.	**MYRA.**	**JEN.**
The economy.	The Local News.	Oligarchies.

CLEO.

...The... patriarchy...?   The government's run out of coins!

RHONDA. It's hard when your man is going through it.

ALYSSA. It really is. And I've been carrying us. Emotionally, financially. And I can't even talk to him about it. I don't want to make him feel any worse than he already does.

(*She's raw, exposed. Tears come.*)

SORRY.

What was I –

We can beat it. *It's just a Game.*

RHONDA. *Yes. YES!*

CLEO. It's just a stupid game! It's not even real!

(**ALYSSA** *is now feeling the community. The connection. She now understands why women sometimes choose to travel together*

*in big packs and share plates of mozzarella
sticks and hold each other's purses. This
feeling energizes her.)*

ALYSSA. *(Galvanized.)* Exactly! It's a world that does
not *exist*. It's a waste of time, and TIME is our most
precious resource as human beings on this planet –

JEN. And water but / YES.

ALYSSA. We will NOT just stand idly by while our life
partners get sucked balls or um, labia-first into the
metaverse. Women of Troy, we will FIGHT. GAME
OVER, GAME!

ALL. YESSSS!!!

CLEO. But – how?

*(They're all looking at **ALYSSA**, expectantly.)*

ALYSSA. *(Still galvanized.)* ...I don't KNOW yet! Ideas.
We need ideas.

(Everyone thinks, then:)

CLEO. We could get the internet shut off! Is there like a
cable, we could cut?

MYRA. I thought it was in – the clouds?

RHONDA. If we didn't have internet, I couldn't check my
Poshmark offers. So, no.

JEN. Yeah, I need the news. ALL OF THE INSTABILITY
KEEPS ME SANE / KEEPING TABS ON IT.

ALYSSA. And I need to work.

(They all think.)

RHONDA. We could take the game thingies –

ALYSSA. Consoles, they're called consoles –

RHONDA. We could hide them!

MYRA. *(Excited.)* Or run them over! With our CARS!

CLEO. Brad would just go out and buy another one.

(Of dip.) What is *in* this dip? I taste something. It's not Greek yogurt.

JEN. Hannah's always trying to get me to quote unquote, hashtag "open up." maybe that's it? Maybe just tell them how we feel?

> *(A moment when they all consider this, then all burst out laughing because it's absurd.)*

Right! That's crazy!

ALYSSA. These are great ideas, though. No such thing as a bad idea, except for that talking one, Jen. Let's keep thinking.

> *(They think again. Eat their little snacks.)*

> *(**CLEO** takes another big bite of dip. Eats.)*

CLEO. *(Of dip.)* Oh, I know what it tastes like! It's Jizz!

> *(They all just look at her. Intrigued, confused.)*

ALYSSA. ...I'm sorry?

RHONDA.	**MYRA**.
Did you say jizz?	What's jazz?

JEN. It's, ah. Ejaculation –

MYRA. Oh! Spunk!

CLEO. *(Embarrassed.)* Sorry. I was just saying this dip tastes like...

> *(Then.)*

Do you guys ever just taste it? Out of nowhere? I do. In ranch dressing. In cream cheese frosting. In my moisturizer. In this dip.

CLEO. Is that weird?

ALL. *(But it's not.)* No, / not at all, that's normal.

JEN. I'm actually not sure.

CLEO. Brad likes it when I –

So I guess I've ingested a lot.

> *(They're all looking at her, worried.)*

But it's okay! I consent! I "CONSENT"!

> *(She knows that's the word she's supposed
> to say.)*

ALYSSA. …It's Greek yogurt.

> (**CLEO** *takes a nervous bite of celery and dip.*)

CLEO. Okay *now* I taste the Greek yogurt!

> *(Suddenly, prompted by this weird moment,*
> **ALYSSA** *gets an idea. She stands.)*

ALYSSA. Wait. THAT'S IT! That's how we beat The Game.
We stop giving them what they want.

MYRA. Dinner?

ALYSSA. Sex. No sex until they stop playing. It's us, or The
Game.

RHONDA. …My question is, will that work?

ALYSSA. Of course it'll work. It's the ultimate weapon.

Ladies, throughout the course of human history –

> *(She clicks and begins another impressive
> PowerPoint display.)*

Women have used sex as leverage to get what they
want, with GREAT success.

(She shows us random images of women in the Bible, Medieval concubines, maybe a few pomegranates. The slides then get more specific, referencing actual sex strikes throughout history.)*

RHONDA. When did you make / this?

ALYSSA. The women's trade union of the Igbo tribe of Nigeria!

Wives and girlfriends of Columbian gang members!

The women of the Liberia Mass Action of Peace!

Alyssa Milano!!!!

Our sexuality isn't a vulnerability. It shouldn't be apologized for. It's our STRENGTH. *We* have the atomic weapon. It's the most powerful of statements, and it contains just a single word: NO.

CLEO. *(Trying it on.)* NO!

ALYSSA. *YES!* This is our mission: NO SEX UNTIL THEY STOP PLAYING THE GAME! WHO'S WITH ME?

RHONDA. Really, though, will they notice?

(They all look at her. Consider this.)

I just feel like Fred – that part of him – might be lost.

(This makes them all sad.)

ALYSSA. I don't accept that.

Then Rhonda, girl, we need to get it BACK. WHO'S WITH ME?!

RHONDA. ...Okay. I'm in.

JEN. ...Sure!

---

* A license to produce *The Game* does not include a license to publicly display any branded logos or trademarked images. Licensees must acquire rights for any logos and/or images or create their own.

MYRA. I'll do it, if it's what everyone wants to do.

ALYSSA. Cleo?

CLEO. I don't know. If I – can. Brad is a very – physical person.

ALYSSA. Of course you can. You gotta hit 'em where it HURTS –

HOMER. Where what hurts?

>   *(Suddenly, **HOMER** is standing in the room, watching all of them.)*
>
>   *(He's come up from downstairs for more snacks.)*
>
>   *(They look at him like he's an ogre, when really, he's just a nice and regular looking guy, just a bit – disheveled.)*
>
>   *(They force smiles, like they're at a zoo and he's on display.)*
>
>   *(**ALYSSA** smiles the most.)*

ALYSSA. *(Brightly.)* Hi honey! These're – my – these are Women! We're doing / the book club –

WOMEN EXCEPT CLEO.	**CLEO.**
Hiiiiiiiiiiii!	BOOK! *WAR AND PEACE*!

HOMER. Oh right! Hi, how are ya?

Thanks for coming, I'm so glad Lys is doing this, something fun for herself. She's been working so freakin' hard.

ALYSSA. I didn't think you'd be up!

HOMER. Oh! Well. I wanted to tell you!

(So excited.) I WON! I beat the big boss! I got farther than I ever have, and then I won! I won a Barrel!

(*They all smile and nod like he's a toddler who just announced that he peed in the potty.*)

ALYSSA. That's so great!

(*Then.*)

What's in it?

HOMER. I don't know yet! That's what's so exciting!

(*He spots the snacks on the table.*)

OOH! Dip.

(*They all watch as he grabs a few pita chips with dip.*)

(**CLEO** *especially watches him eat.*)

(**HOMER** *suddenly feels like he doesn't belong.*)

Welp! Back to the grind!

Nice to you meet you.

(*He spots the baby strapped to* **ALYSSA**.)

Be good to your Mama.

ALYSSA. Love you!

(*He kisses the baby's head.*)

(*He heads back downstairs.*)

MYRA. (*Sotto, to* **RHONDA**.) That baby is an angel.

RHONDA. It's kinda weird.

(**ALYSSA** *faces them, desperate.*)

ALYSSA. ...Please. I need my husband back. I can't do this alone.

(*All eyes are on* **CLEO**.)

CLEO. I guess I could – try –

ALYSSA. GREAT! We're united! No more sex. I think this'll take, what? Twenty-four hours?

RHONDA. More like twenty-four *MINUTES*!

CLEO. Twenty-four *Seconds*!

(*They all laugh again.*)

RHONDA. Can we still flick it?

ALYSSA. Um – I guess I don't see why not?

MYRA. Let's make a pact!

ALYSSA. YES!

(**MYRA** *takes the knife out of the cheese.*)

(*Cuts her finger. They all shriek as some blood drips out.*)

MYRA. ...Oh, we're not doing blood?

ALYSSA. No, I think just the wine is good! Would you like a – napkin?

MYRA. Yes, thank you.

(**ALYSSA** *hands her a beverage napkin to wrap around her finger.*)

(*She then holds out an open bottle of Chardonnay.*)

ALYSSA. Repeat after me.

I will not have sex with my husband.

(*To* **JEN**.) Partner. Sorry.

ALL EXCEPT JEN.	**JEN.**
I will not have sex with my husband.	I will not have sex with my partner.

ALYSSA. Even if he does something really thoughtful. Even if he *begs. Even* if he just got out of the shower – and he's very wet, and it's very hot –

> (**CLEO** *is quiet.*)

Cleo?

CLEO. …Even if he just got out of the shower.

MYRA. *(Amped.)* I will MASTURBATE!

ALYSSA. WHATEVER IT TAKES.

> (*She takes a swig from a bottle of lukewarm Chardonnay.*)
>
> (*Passes it along. One by one, they all drink, except for* **CLEO** *who just pretends to, and giggles.*)

May their loins be lonely – Let's do a circle thing –

> (*They all start to walk in a weird circle, like a ritual.*)

JEN. What're we doing? Okay –

ALYSSA. May they long for us.

May they remember who we are.

> (*They all raise their glasses, and they drink.*)

Bundles

(**RHONDA**, *wearing ridiculous clothes.*)

RHONDA. Okay. I'm gonna teach you how to use Poshmark.

Go to your closet. Open it up. Look at all of your damn clothes.

Why do you have all of those clothes?! Because you wanted to *feel* a certain way. Or be a certain type of person. Sexy, or adventurous, or "lithe," that's why I bought this purple snake print capri-length compression spacetech activewear lounge skort.

(*She shows it to us on her phone.*)

I wore it once. Sold it the next day for three bucks more than I paid for it. Flipped that skort like a house.

Whoever you wanted to be, whatever made you buy denim underwear, you're not that person anymore! So sell the clothes to somebody else so that *they* can try and be someone *they're* not!

You need to wear what you love so that you love yourself. What was that thing my mom used to always say? Beauty comes from the *outside*.

I don't get people who don't care about clothes! The right pants can get you back a whole *feeling* that's been lost. My husband still has the same sweatshirt from the pizza place he worked at in college, which was about the last time we kissed on the mouth. He doesn't care what he looks like. Well, I care. *I care* what I look like. But I could walk into the room in a men's clown suit and he would not notice. And I know, because I tried. And it wasn't Halloween y'all, this was like a regular day in March.

And the man barely looked up!

(This makes her sad. She pushes through.)

So. Once you've found the clothes you want to sell, take flattering pictures of each item. Post on Poshmark. Sell to the highest bidder.

Then – this is the best part – buy something new for yourself.

Find out who you want to be next.

Try a scoop neck. Or a mini skirt. Or wide leg. Or kitten heel. Figure out who you are. WHO ARE YOU?

ARE YOU FUN? ARE YOU BEAUTIFUL? ARE YOU ALIVE?!

OR ARE YOU INVISIBLE?

Don't be that. Be someone else.

Whoever that is.

(Emotion swells. She avoids. Scrolls through Poshmark listings on her phone.)

Men Will Be Men Will Be Men

(Later that night.)

(The basement. It reeks of farts and dreams and Bagel Bites.)

*(**HOMER** plays The Game.)*

HOMER. Errghhhh this guy's such a bullet sponge!

No, watch the back. He's coming up the side, he's coming up the side!!!!!!!

(He transitions to a more gentle, conversational tone.)

Oh, hey, did you talk to your dad?

FUCK THAT GUY! Not your dad. The guy on the right.

I'm gonna camp up here and see who I can smoke.

I get it dude. He wants that security for you, and MBA is a great track, but if you really wanna do the poetry major, now's the time to go for it. You've gotta trust your gut, that's the life lesson you really get in college, you become your own person, and you start to *trust* that person. You have to. I'm telling you dude, you're living the best years of your life.

Ah, I majored in engineering.

Yeah, dude, I was the MAN in college. Now I'm just – *a* Man.

(It saddens him a bit. He keeps playing The Game.)

YOU GOT 'IM!

Oh shit!

*(They play. **ALYSSA** enters.)*

Hey, pretty lady!

(Into game.) BRB.

(To **ALYSSA**.*)* You need a break, want me to take the baby?

ALYSSA. Baby's asleep.

HOMER. Great. How was the book club?

ALYSSA. Good! It was good.

HOMER. Really? You had a good time?

ALYSSA. Yeah! Why?

HOMER. You hate large groups of women.

ALYSSA. I don't "hate" large groups of women! I just – prefer – smaller, more intimate interactions.

HOMER. I think it's awesome you're making friends.

ALYSSA. I have friends! My mom is my friend!

HOMER. And me. I'm your friend.

> *(This warms* **ALYSSA**. *He's so sweet. It kills her.)*

ALYSSA. Hey, you know I love you, right?

HOMER. Yeah! No der. Love you too.

ALYSSA. I actually - need to -

> *(She quickly consults the video game terms handout that she passed around earlier.)*

I need to – "cutscene" with you.

HOMER. ...What?

ALYSSA. I have something to say to you, / and the thing I have to say is actually – an ultimatum.

HOMER. That's not at all what a cutscene is.

...Okay?

ALYSSA. I'm going to say this clearly, and with confidence –

HOMER. I think you're doing great so far.

ALYSSA. Thanks honey.

(A breath, then.)

I don't want to make a big thing about this, but I've actually become really concerned about the amount of time you spend down here playing The Game –

*(**HOMER**'s eyes float back to The Game. He starts to play again.)*

…and I've tried talking to you about it and you've told me on multiple occasions that you're going to try and cut back and maybe start swimming again, or volunteer? Or even just get dinner going, like you used to – are you playing right now?

HOMER. Sorry. My buddy's on.

Dinner! Yes! I was thinking about trying Blue Apron! / I got a coupon –

ALYSSA. I don't want to do any Aprons! I want you to stop playing The Game!

(Then.)

I'm worried about you. It can't be good for you to play this much.

*(**HOMER** seems embarrassed.)*

HOMER. No, um. Yeah. I could stop.

ALYSSA. *(Hopeful.)* Really? You could?

HOMER. Is there something you need me to do that I'm not doing? I make the bed, I take out the trash, I make sweet sweet love to you –

ALYSSA. Yes, I love all of that, but lately –

HOMER. What?

ALYSSA. You don't – take any *initiative.* / I'm sorry. That's a shitty word.

HOMER. Right.

ALYSSA. I'm just saying you could use this time! You're on unemployment! You could start a nonprofit! Or build a – shed!

HOMER. Why would I build a shed?

ALYSSA. To put things in!

HOMER. Like –

ALYSSA. *(Searching, then.)* ...Mulch...?

HOMER. I'm not hurting anyone.

ALYSSA. You're hurting you. Which hurts me.

HOMER. It's just a Game.

(Beat.)

ALYSSA. ...Well, then, I guess, there's nothing left to say, or do.

(Then.)

Except this. Here it comes.

(She gathers confidence, then, with force:)

No more sex. It's either me or The Game.

*(**HOMER** laughs. Then realizes she's serious. So he stops laughing.)*

*(**HOMER** considers this. **ALYSSA** watches him closely as he considers.)*

HOMER. ...Oh. / You're serious. Hmm –

ALYSSA. ..."Oh"?

HOMER. I'm just – I'm / processing –

ALYSSA. Wow.

HOMER. Of course I choose you! / This is stupid.

ALYSSA. Do you think I'm kidding?

HOMER. No –

ALYSSA. Because I'm not, Homer.

(With bravado.) NO MORE SEX.

HOMER. This is ridiculous. You can't blackmail me. I'm not doing this.

ALYSSA. No, Homer. You're not doing THIS.

(Then.)

Myself. I mean you're not doing myself. Me. You're not / doing me.

HOMER. Yeah, I got that.

ALYSSA. You can't touch my boobs, either.

These. Remember these?

(She shows him her breasts, defiantly.)

HOMER. Yeah, I saw them this morning, when you were doing your back stretches. I see them every day.

ALYSSA. Okay, well. No more of these!

(He hears Marcio talking to him through his headset.)

HOMER. Yep, I'm here!

(He puts his headset back on.)

(Plays The Game. Defiantly.)

ALYSSA. Homer.

(No response.)

Homer.

(He plays.)

(She looks at him in disbelief. Sadly, she puts her boobs away.)

(Slowly moves away from him.)

*(Suddenly, **ALYSSA** is alone.)*

*(She looks back to **HOMER**.)*

(Gets out her phone.)

CLEO. Hi! I made us a groupchat so we can text!

(A text chain begins, a chorus of pleasantries and emojis and overshares. It builds like a symphony, lighting up phones like a drive-through Christmas lights display. Each light brings a ping of dopamine.)

Like!

(I Hope you Enjoy this article I found on BuzzFeed: "Ten Ways to Know Your Husband Still Loves You.")

JEN. *(Overthinking.)* Dot dot dot

CLEO. (I hope you like this article I read on Glitterpuss: "Thirteen Budget-friendly Ways to Clean Your Vagina.")

JEN. Dot dot dot

CLEO. (I Hope you like this Quiz I just took: "How to Know if You're Using the Internet to Find New Reasons to be Mad at Yourself.")

JEN. *(Overthinking.)* Dot dot dot

Dot dot dot

RHONDA. Ooh, could y'all help me out and like my Athleisure bundle on Poshmark? Here's the link. Does anyone need a Skort?

MYRA. Hello, I

> *(She struggles to type on her keyboard, keeps hitting send by accident. Everyone waits.)*

'm

I'm

'm

Happy 2 B here

> *(She smiles as she sends the text. Feels proud. She truly, truly is happy to be here.)*

RHONDA. Yay Myra! You did that!

CLEO & JEN. Haha

MYRA. Where is the – there it is.

Laughing crying face!

ALYSSA. How's everyone's week going? Any luck?

RHONDA.	**CLEO.**	**MYRA.**
Nadda	Nope	Frowny face.

> *(**ALYSSA** considers. She looks back to **HOMER**, who's playing The Game.)*

> *(She feels so alone.)*

ALYSSA. Does anyone want to come over tomorrow night?

RHONDA.	**CLEO.**	**MYRA.**
I'm in.	YES!	Yes please!

> *(Finally, **JEN** responds.)*

JEN. Dot dot dot

Dot dot dot

(Then, with courage.)

…I'll be there. Yay.

(This is hard for her.)

Smiley face.

(The smiley face makes all of them smile.)

Women Helping Women Helping Women Helping Women

(**JEN** *hovers, looking through pictures on her camera.*)

(*She's frozen until we click on her. Click.*)

(*She then clicks through pictures on her camera. Deleting some, keeping some.*)

(*Some of them terrify her.*)

(*Some of them make her proud.*)

(*After a few moments:*)

JEN. Fun fact about me! I got my first period at the Holocaust museum in Washington, D.C.! Yep. I was just standing there looking at those horrible piles of shoes. And then just –

(*She mimes a gush of blood.*)

Checked into the Red Roof Inn for the foreseeable future. And now every month, for the last...seventeen years? I wake up one morning and I hate everything, but at the same time everything is so beautiful, and I feel to connected to my ancestors and I REALLY want SunChips and I think *God, I'm so profound and alive, and is there something wrong with me, do I have a brain tumor? Am I a genius?!*

And then I get my period.

And I remember I'm a woman.

And then I think about those shoes.

(*Clicks through.*)

I've always avoided things that involve large groups of women because it's just a lot of everyone asking for a little box for their leftovers. And that thing where the periods sync up, that just seems like witchcraft to me. No thank you. But I've always had Hannah.

(Then.)

We've been together eight years. Before her, I kissed a lot of women who turned out NOT to be into girls, like basically women used me to determine they were in fact straight. Though I like to think they lie awake next to their husbands, imagining me.

So Hannah's been my first real, and longest, gig. Relationship. She's a second grade teacher and she's just very open, like her heart is on her sleeve and mine's like, buried beneath like, eight fleeces and also a weighted blanket.

(Clicks through.)

She's this really naturally happy and open person, she's got this joy that's infectious and she infects me with it. If she has a cold, she gives me that too.

Hannah says I need to be more "vulnerable," open myself up to connections with people outside of our relationship, and I'm like lady, you are all I need.

But a few months ago, a kid brought a gun to her school.

No one was hurt, Thank God, but she had to lock her classroom door, get the kids in the middle. The whole deal. It really shook her up. The kid who brought the gun to school, he used to be in Hannah's class. She says it doesn't make sense to her. She says nothing makes sense to her anymore. Except The Game, I guess.

(She clicks.)

(She finds the picture she's looking for. It's of Hannah.)

Hereeeeee it is. Here's Hannah. This one's my favorite of her.

She's smiling in this one.

(She shows it to us.)

Beauty Pie 10-Minute Miracle Hydrating Sheet Mask

(Back in the living room.)

*(The **WOMEN** are gathered, once again. It's a week later.)*

(They're a bit more comfortable around each other, this time.)

(They all wear sheet face masks, their eyes blinking weirdly through the holes. Conversing is hard with the masks on their faces, but they're all trying.)

*(**JEN** still snaps the occasional picture, careful not to get mask goo on her lens.)*

RHONDA. Thanks so much for the face masks!

ALYSSA. I thought they'd be fun! I don't know. I don't really know what women do together.

We should have music! Alexa play – Taylor Swift. Wait, no. Don't. ALEXA STOP.

CLEO. *(To **ALYSSA**.)* Where's the baby?

ALYSSA. Oh, he's in his box.

RHONDA. His –?

ALYSSA. His bed.

JEN. *(Of masks.)* What's in this? It kind of stings.

ALYSSA. ...Avocado, I think?

RHONDA. *(Of mask.)* It smells good! Smells like – what does it smell like?

<table>
<tr><td>CLEO.</td><td>ALYSSA.</td></tr>
<tr><td>Flowers.</td><td>Diamonds.</td></tr>
<tr><td>JEN.</td><td>RHONDA.</td></tr>
<tr><td>A fresh perspective.</td><td>Peach sparkling water?</td></tr>
<tr><td></td><td>MYRA.</td></tr>
<tr><td>Middle School.</td><td>Cookies!</td></tr>
</table>

ALYSSA. *(Reading the face mask packet.)* They're supposed to smell like "Young Water."

(They all agree, Oh, yeah, that's it.)

MYRA. How long do we leave them on for?

ALYSSA. Three and a half more minutes.

(Then.)

I don't do this enough. Spend time with other women.

JEN. Me neither.

ALYSSA. I have my friends from college! We just live all over the place. And our lives are so crazy, it's hard to find a time we can all get together. We're planning a trip to Napa, in 2040! I'm excited.

RHONDA. You *have* to make time for your girlfriends. It's *so* important.

JEN. And turmeric, too! Fixes everything.

MYRA. This is my first time doing a face mask!

ALYSSA. Ever?! Your skin is incredible!

MYRA. I always just do what my mother did. Oil of Olay in the morning, and at night.

RHONDA. It's so important we take this time to take care of ourselves like this, and not feel guilty about it.

ALYSSA. I wake up feeling guilty every morning, for just existing.

CLEO. My mom says my first word was "sorry."

JEN.	**ALYSSA.**	**RHONDA.**
Oh my God. That's *horrible*.	Wow.	The Patriarchy.

JEN. The last time I washed my face was because there was peanut butter on it.

RHONDA. I do a mask every night. Self-care is *survival*. That's what Almond says.

CLEO. Who's Almond?

RHONDA. She's the new Peloton Teacher. She used to be a Supreme Court Justice! She left to become an inspirational fitness celebrity.

JEN. Aren't those bikes thousands of dollars?

RHONDA. There's a payment plan! I'm going to pay five dollars a month for thirty-five years.

(To **JEN**.*)* You should get one!

JEN. Oh, I'm not home much. I travel a lot, for work.

ALYSSA. What is it that you do for work?

JEN. I'm a photographer.

CLEO. Do you do newborns?!

JEN. ...No.

(They all just look at her, expectantly.)

(Mumbling.) I'm a war photographer.

ALYSSA. What was that?

JEN. *(Louder.)* I take pictures of War.

CLEO. *(Sweet, clueless.)* Why?

JEN. So that we know they're happening. Otherwise, we forget.

JEN. I can show you – if you want –

(She shows them images on her camera. They gather to look at them. The pictures sober them.)

ALYSSA. I do forget, sometimes.

CLEO. Brad never talks about it. So I don't ask.

MYRA. ...Those poor people.

RHONDA. This *world*.

*(She reaches for **JEN**'s hand.)*

*(Just then, **HOMER** appears in the doorway.)*

HOMER. What about the world?

(They all turn and look at him at the exact same time, blinking weirdly through their face masks, it's terrifying.)

AHHHH!

WOMEN. AHHHHH!!!!!!

*(**ALYSSA** slides hers off, self-conscious.)*

ALYSSA. ...Hi.

HOMER. Did you turn the air off?

ALYSSA. I don't know. I might have.

(They're talking nicely, but the passive-aggressive tension between them is palpable.)

HOMER. It's kinda stuffy down in the basement.

ALYSSA. We feel fine up here.

HOMER. I'm going to turn it back on.

ALYSSA. Go for it. It's your house.

HOMER. Is it?

ALYSSA. What?

>   (**HOMER** *adjust the A/C. Heads back to the door.)*

Could you shut the door please?

HOMER. When I go back downstairs, yes. I will shut the door. But right now, I'm still in the room. So, no.

ALYSSA. I don't mean right now. I mean when you *go.*

>   (**HOMER** *just stands there, just to piss her off.)*

HOMER. Well, now I'm going. Because I want to.

>   *(Then, he goes back down. Shutting the door behind him.)*

>   (**ALYSSA** *is embarrassed.)*

ALYSSA. Sorry about – that. That was so awkward. We don't usually fight like that.

JEN. *(To **RHONDA**.) That* was a fight?

RHONDA. *(To **JEN**.)* For white people yes.

ALYSSA. I thought I'd deliver the ultimatum, and that'd be that, but he'd rather play The Game than have sex with me. And I found out I'm up for a HUGE new sustainable retail space project, which is what I've basically been working towards for the last twenty years –

RHONDA.	CLEO.	JEN.	MYRA.
You *go!*	That's amazing!	Nice!	Yippee!!

ALYSSA. Thank you! I should feel powerful and accomplished but my husband is mad at me so instead I feel needy, and sad, and alone.

>   *(Her phone alarm goes off.)*

ALYSSA. Ten minutes! Masks off! Fun.

>*(They all slide their masks off.)*

MYRA. You're not alone, dear.

>**(MYRA** *places a hand on her.)*

>**(ALYSSA***'s grateful for it.)*

ALYSSA. Thank you. It's been a really hard week.

RHONDA. Why?

>*(Then.)*

OH! Right. For me too!

CLEO. And for me!

MYRA. I'll say the same thing, too.

JEN. Jumping on here! *Yes!*

CLEO. Yeah, it's been really – hard!

MYRA. Right, Right! It's difficult!

RHONDA. Tough titties, tough times!

>*(The other* **WOMEN** *all look at each other, sussing each other out.)*

>**(ALYSSA** *realizes something.)*

ALYSSA. You all had sex, didn't you?!

JEN. I'm sorry!

CLEO. I had to!

RHONDA. The Celtics won the playoffs! Fred was so happy! It's the one night a year that I get some!

JEN. I told Hannah no sex, just cuddling.

But then we cuddled.

And had sex. She needed me –

ALYSSA. Cleo?

CLEO. Sex is Brad and I's love language!

MYRA. My love language is English!

CLEO. ...We do it every day.

<table>
<tr><td>JEN.</td><td>RHONDA.</td></tr>
<tr><td>Every day?!</td><td>Even week days?!</td></tr>
<tr><td>On purpose?</td><td>ALYSSA.</td></tr>
<tr><td></td><td>Aren't you tired?</td></tr>
</table>

CLEO. *(Blushing, but proud.)* Sometimes twice in one day.

ALYSSA.   TWICE? WHY? WHY WOULD YOU DO THAT? YOU ARE PREGNANT.

CLEO. Because we love each other.

ALYSSA. ...Huh.

JEN. That's really sweet.

> *(This lands on the* **WOMEN**. *Sex is Love, or it can be. We forget that, but it is.)*

RHONDA. Good for you. Get it while you can.

CLEO. It's going to change? After the baby?

RHONDA. *(Laughs, then –)* Oh, yes. In...all ways. All of them.

ALYSSA. Myra – did you?

MYRA. Hmm?

ALYSSA. Did you have sex with your – Mark?

MYRA. Oh! No, dear.

ALYSSA. THANK you!

MYRA. Because he's dead.

ALYSSA. WHAT?!

RHONDA.	**CLEO**.	**JEN**.
OH MY GOD!	He died?!	Jesus!
	When?	

MYRA. Oh! Oh, I'm fine. He's been dead for some time, now. He had a heart attack, three years ago.

ALYSSA. ...So wait, then why are you here?

MYRA. Hmm?

ALYSSA. Why did you join this group? For people who've lost partners to The Game.

MYRA. Oh, Well. I've started seeing a new doctor for my arthritis, and when I was filling out the forms, they asked for an "in case of emergency contact" and I realized I had no one to put down.

I had friends! They're just all gone, now.

So I went on Facebook, to find some new ones.

(Then.)

Please don't kick me out!

CLEO. We can't kick Myra out!! We need Myra!!

ALYSSA. There's nothing to kick you out of, this is not a formal / entity.

RHONDA. *(To **MYRA**, comforting.)* No one's kicking you out.

*(**ALYSSA** sits, frustrated. Puts her head in her hands.)*

ALYSSA. So you all had sex? Except for me.

MYRA. Oh, I didn't –

ALYSSA. Not you, Myra. Those of you who – physically could.

(They all nod guiltily.)

ALYSSA. So did they stop playing The Game?

(**CLEO** *and* **JEN** *shake their heads no, ashamed.*)

RHONDA. We did it while The Game was paused.

ALYSSA. But Homer didn't even want –

(*She contemplates this.*)

So maybe I'm the problem?

(**CLEO** *raises her hand.*)

You really don't have to raise your hand.

CLEO. Is it okay to...with our husbands again?

ALYSSA. Sure. Fine. Let's just give up.

RHONDA. We can't give up! Fred bought adult diapers!

JEN. Oh, God.

CLEO. Why?

RHONDA. DO THE MATH, CLEO.

JEN. Hannah's really not okay. I don't wanna give up. We just need a new plan.

ALYSSA. Okay, if it's *not* sex, then what is it they need that we can legally withhold?

CLEO. (*Sweetly.*) Blowjobs?

ALYSSA. Honey, I think we're brainstorming things other than sex.

JEN. Honestly, I couldn't tell you what men need, other than to be left alone, but that was maybe just my dad.

MYRA. What're we talking about?

ALYSSA. What men need. Other than sex.

MYRA. Oh, well. Mark was always happiest when he was organizing the garage.

MYRA. Fixing a hole in the roof.

Maybe they just need something to *do*!

(**ALYSSA** *processes this.*)

ALYSSA. Yes. Myra. *Yes.* They need *Purpose.*

CLEO. That's why Brad joined the army! He said he wanted to actually *do* something with his life!

ALYSSA. If men don't feel a sense of purpose, they don't feel like *men*! They're finding purpose in The Game! We need to give them purpose again, in the real world.

JEN. This feels like a generalization? But – / no, yeah, continue.

(**ALYSSA** *finds her PowerPoint clicker somewhere, click, another elaborate presentation comes down.*)

RHONDA. BOOM! Another PowerPoint! I love this lady!

ALYSSA. SINCE THE DAWN OF MAN, he has needed Purpose. A reason to get out of bed. A family to feed, an enemy to defeat, a driveway full of leaves to clear!

(*Pictures of treehouses, leaves being raked into a pile. Stacks of paperwork, bloody battles, extra strength garbage bags!*)

We need to give them something more meaningful to *do*!

Are you done with that plate?

(*She starts to clean up.*)

RHONDA. But I already do everything.

ALYSSA. Of course you do, Rhonda. We always do everything. You'll have to *not* do something, *on purpose.*

JEN. Seems passive aggressive –

ALYSSA. Women aren't allowed to be the regular kind of aggressive unless we're playing SPORTS!

(Then.)

NEW PLAN.

(Her PowerPoint continues. Graphs, pictures of large phallic buildings, crowded sports arenas, Corvettes, Hungry Man microwavable dinners, crowns.)

We'll make them feel useful, again, thus filling them with a sense of PRIDE, which will restore BALANCE!

(To **JEN**.*)* And maybe it'll work for Hannah, too!

JEN. You really don't have to / keep doing that.

ALYSSA. *(Resuming.)* LADIES, TO YOUR BATTLE STATIONS I MEAN YOUR HOUSES.

(They retreat to their houses like they're preparing for battle. From somewhere, the **WOMEN** *procure and hand* **ALYSSA** *a giant fish.)*

*(***ALYSSA*** is left alone, in the living room.)*

(She clears her throat. Finds her smallest, sweetest, most innocent voice.)

...Homer?

(Suddenly, all of the **WOMEN** *are gone.)*

(It's later. Much later.)

(The house is empty, cold. Dim light.)

(Sweetly.) Hey, Homey?

(After a few moments, **HOMER** *comes upstairs.)*

HOMER. Yeah?

ALYSSA. Sorry about the air thing, earlier.

(He keeps his guard up.)

HOMER. It's okay. I was being a turd, too.

ALYSSA. We're both not our best selves right now. There's a lot going on. With the baby –

HOMER. Yeah. It's a lot.

ALYSSA. I know you don't like to talk about it / but. I'm sorry you lost your job.

HOMER. I have a game paused –

ALYSSA. No, listen. It wasn't your fault. It was just a shitty thing that happened. You were there for ten years. It's a big change. You're allowed to be hurt, and angry, and take whatever time you need to feel all that.

HOMER. *(Truly.)* Thanks. That's actually really nice to hear.

ALYSSA. I mean it. I'm sorry.

(She kisses him.)

(She rests on him for a moment.)

Oh, hey, Can you do something for me? The garbage disposal's making a weird sound –

HOMER. *(Galvanized.)* Probably a fork. Madam, say no more. I got you. The garbage disposal is no match for my calloused man hands!!!!

(He heads off to the kitchen.)

*(***ALYSSA** *stands, waits.)*

*(Offstage, the sound of a kitchen war, a garbage disposal grinding and grinding itself. Blades slicing against other metals. **HOMER** curses indistinguishably.)*

*(**ALYSSA** winces.)*

*(After a few moments, **HOMER** returns, looking like he's been to battle.)*

(There might be meat juice in his hair.)

(He's holding a Mangled Fish Skeleton.)

*(He holds it out to **ALYSSA**.)*

Did you...put a fish down the drain?

ALYSSA. *(Caught.)* I don't know.

HOMER. Where did you get this – what kind of fish is this?

ALYSSA. It's a rainbow trout! But I've never seen that before.

HOMER. ...I don't need your pity.

ALYSSA. I'm sorry, I'm just trying to help you feel – like yourself again –

HOMER. By breaking our house?

ALYSSA. You just – you seem a little lost –

*(**HOMER** knows he's completely lost. But he doesn't want to admit it.)*

HOMER. *(Defensive.)* I'm – in transition.

ALYSSA. You'd rather play a Game than have sex with your wife!

HOMER. No, I just refuse to be blackmailed.

How about this. A trade. I'll stop playing The Game if you give me your phone.

(Beat.)

ALYSSA. *What?* No.

HOMER. Why not?

ALYSSA. *I need my phone.* For work. This game is not your livelihood.

HOMER. I just like it! Okay? I enjoy it!

ALYSSA. Well, how do you think it makes me feel? When people ask what you're up to – and I don't know what to *say – He plays this video game for ninety hours a week. He wins barrels!*

HOMER. So that's what this is about? What other people think?

(A moment, because it's true.)

ALYSSA. *(Gently.)* ...I ...I want to feel proud of you, and I don't right now.

(This hurts.)

That's not what I want to say.

Just – talk to me, Homer.

(Beat.)

HOMER. I *know* it's just a Game. But it's what I have going on right now. Okay?

ALYSSA. I just – I feel like that's a choice.

I was talking to the book club gals about your current – employment situation / and –

HOMER. You talked to them about me?

ALYSSA. I have to talk to SOMEONE, Homer.

HOMER. *(Scoffing.)* Okay. Great.

(He starts to go.)

ALYSSA. It's not real. *The Game's not real!*

HOMER. *(Hard.)* It's the realest thing in my life right now.

ALYSSA. Okay. Well, I have skin, and I breathe air, and I have internal organs, and so I don't know how to be any more...*real.*

(*A moment.*)

HOMER. Why didn't you tell me you were up for that new project?

(**ALYSSA** *is caught.*)

I heard you on that call the other night.

ALYSSA. I – I didn't want to make you feel bad.

HOMER. Well, that makes me feel *really* bad.

(*Then.*)

I have to get back to The Game.

ALYSSA. No. You *don't.*

HOMER. Actually, yeah I do. I'm trying to beat the level before the EP drops.

ALYSSA. EP?

HOMER. There's a new version of The Game. Coming out Friday. Beta version of the Expansion Pack. Invite only.

(*Then.*)

But everyone's invited.

(*He goes.*)

(**ALYSSA** *is alone again.*)

(*She sends a text to the* **WOMEN.**)

(*Another chorus of texts begins.*)

ALYSSA. *(Shouting.)* ATTN: WOMEN. WE HAVE A SITUATION.

JEN. Oh no! What?

RHONDA. Did you wear black and navy to work because that's fine now.

JEN. Was it ever not fine?

CLEO. Are you guys mad at me? What'd I do?

ALYSSA. ...No one is mad at you, Cleo.

MYRA. This came up on the iPad! Hello? Are you there?

I was hoping to hear from you all today!

ALYSSA. WE HAVE A HUGE HUGE PROBLEM.

MYRA. *(Shouting.)* WHY ARE WE SHOUTING?

ALYSSA. *(Shouting.)* I JUST HAVE THE CAPS LOCK ON, FOR EMPHASIS. EMERGENCY MEETING AT MY HOUSE.

JEN.	**RHONDA**.	**CLEO**.
Thumbs up	I'll be there	Yay!

MYRA. Can I bring anything? I could make a Bundt!

Can I do anything?

Hello?

Hello?

*(But the text chain has gone silent, everyone was sucked back into their lives. **MYRA** is left alone.)*

Okay. Goodbye! With love, Myra.

(She puts her phone away.)

(She is somehow even more alone.)

Her Monthly

MYRA. You know, it used to be that women weren't *allowed* to have feelings. Now we have so MANY, I feel crushed by them, by all of the feelings I'm supposed to have. I went to the beauty parlor to get my nails done, and there was a purple I liked. It was called *Eve's Rage*. I didn't like that. So I chose Clear.

My Mother, my Grandmother too – they felt *nothing*, or at least nothing they'd say out loud. They just pounded dough and sometimes disappeared to the grocery store. But the Men were at least allowed the big, steel feelings. Anger and frustration. As long as they felt them in the Garage, or while smoking a cigarette, it was fine.

But not women. When they had their Monthly, they could take an aspirin or an afternoon nap. There was no place for their pain or their grief.

And this is why when I found out I was unable to have children, I at first didn't realize I had permission to feel anything about it! I was raised to ask permission before I did *anything*! *Mother May I, Yes You May.*

I thought that I was just meant to soldier on through the pain, because that's what women do. So I just kept on. I started growing my tomatoes, and I became a librarian. Mark didn't mind that we didn't have children. He never made me feel like I was less than, and I loved him for that. And then years passed, and the children at the library, they were mine.

But they grew up. Moved away.

And then, Mark died. And then one by one, all of my friends died too, my friends from church and my friends from girlhood and my friends from water aerobics.

(Realizing.) Everyone I know is dead.

    (Then.)

Maybe this is why people have children.

Oh, well!

That's what my Mother used to say.

Oh, Well!

...Oh, Well.

Open Crotch Fishnet and Lace Body Stocking

(The **WOMEN** *are gathered again.)*

(There's now more of a closeness between them. A sisterhood forming.)

(Once again, **ALYSSA** *is wearing her baby in an Ergobaby carrier on her chest.)*

(She has a giant box full of plastic packages next to her.)

(She seems a bit unhinged, if not more so than usual.)

(The **WOMEN** *chat amongst themselves, because* **ALYSSA***'s wrapping up a work call, while bouncing a fussing Phillip in his carrier, while refilling someone's wine.)*

JEN. *(To* **RHONDA**, *of her phone.)* What do I do? should I make an offer?

ALYSSA. *(Wrapping up call, calmly.)*
What do you mean, dinosaurs? Like their bones? Well call a museum to come and move them. The pool needs to go in the center. I need to stay on good terms with this client. Like a dinosaur museum, Carly. I have the investors up my ass in places my husband has never been.

RHONDA. *(To* **JEN**.)*
YES! Do it, do it / NOW! This seller's items don't last long!

ALYSSA. *(Then, brightly.)* Hi to your Mom!

(*She hangs up, stressed.*)

(To everyone.) Sorry, sorry. We can start.

(Phillip cries.)

JEN. Okay – okay – how much do I bid?

RHONDA. You gotta start low. It's like what Michelle Obama says. If YOU go low, and then they will ALSO go low.

(**JEN** *works her phone, then:*)

JEN. I did it – I did it!! I made my first offer on Poshmark!!!

RHONDA. *(Tearing up.)* Girl!

(Phillip cries.)

ALYSSA. It's okay –

(Singing.)

BAA BAA BLACK SHEEP –

CLEO. Is he okay?

ALYSSA. Oh! Yep. He's just crying.

MYRA. *(To **ALYSSA**.)* What is it? What's the big problem?!

ALYSSA. There's a new level of The Game dropping this week. A Beta something. All of our partners will have access. And I researched the new level. It has ENDLESS WORLDS AND OUTCOMES.

JEN. Are you serious?

ALYSSA. *Free instant download.*

*(Suddenly, **RHONDA**, who's been looking at her phone, Shrieks!)*

AHHH, What, what?!

RHONDA. I GOT THE DRESS!

> *(They're all just looking at her.)*

The limited edition 2008 Diane Von Furstenberg Periwinkle WRAP DRESS!!!! I had one just like it when I met Fred! I've been trying to find it! And I WON!

> *(She shows it to whoever's closest to her.)*

ALYSSA. Great! Can we focus back on The Game, please?

CLEO. So wait…The Game is never going to end?

ALYSSA. Apparently not. But I have a new plan.

RHONDA. I thought we were doing the "make them feel more useful around the house" plan?

ALYSSA. Did that actually work for anyone?

CLEO. Brad helped me put the crib together!

But then he just went right back downstairs.

For three days.

JEN. I told Hannah that I needed help getting some noodles off the top shelf, but I forgot she was shorter than me.

RHONDA. I told Fred I needed his help opening a jar of pickles but he sprained his wrist and had to go to urgent care, so actually you owe me four hundred dollars.

MYRA. Do you / need an emergency contact?

ALYSSA. Bitches, it's about to get so much worse. Sorry I just called you Bitches.

> *(The baby cries.)*

You're okay!

(She starts to sing a classic love song as an unexpected lullaby.)*

JEN. We're supposed to Spring Clean this weekend.

ALYSSA. YOU'RE NOT CLEANING OUT ANY CABINETS, JEN.

This EP comes out Friday, so we have until Friday to end their addiction, once and for all.

(She digs into the box, holds up a crotchless body stocking in a stiff package.)

NEW NEW PLAN:

(She clicks a remote and the PowerPoint screen starts to come down.)

RHONDA. There she goes! I knew it was coming!

ALYSSA. Instead of no sex, – you can all sit down now – we're going to have *so much sex with them* that they forget about The Game altogether.

(She clicks, a single slide appears.)

PHASE 3: DO LOTS OF SEX.

CLEO. ...Are there any pictures?

ALYSSA. No, Cleo, you horndog, I did not put porn in my PowerPoint. You can use your imagination.

This is the new plan. I'm talking twenty-four seven, *non-stop, sex.*

RHONDA. Can we take power naps?

---

* A license to produce *The Game* does not include a performance license for any third-party or copyrighted music. Licensees should create an original composition or use music in the public domain. For further information, please see the Music and Third-Party Materials Use Note on page iii.

ALYSSA. That's a great question, because I'm already tired just thinking about it. So *yes*.

Okay! Here we go! I have weapons for everyone! I mean little outfits.

(**ALYSSA** *tosses a bag at each of the* **WOMEN**.)

Open them, open them!!!

(The baby cries.)

Not now, Phillip, Mom's doing something.

(They all open their packages.)

(They've each been gifted with a piece of shoddily-made lingerie.)

(A maternity bustier for **CLEO**.*)*

(A chemise for **RHONDA**.*)*

(Weirdly, a little maid costume for **MYRA**.*)*

Myra, I wanted to get you something sensible! Just for fun.

MYRA. *(So honored.)* I didn't get you anything!

ALYSSA. Oh, I got everyone something.

MYRA. I'll wear it when I clean out the fridge!

CLEO. Cute! I hope Brad likes it!

(**CLEO** *starts to put it on over her clothes.)*

ALYSSA. Yes you can resell it on Poshmark. SO all we have to do is seduce them! How hard can that be?

(**JEN** *studies the two packages in her hand. One is a sexy little corset, the other is fully a strap-on penis.)*

(**CLEO** *starts to giggle, embarrassed.*)

RHONDA. Oh, hello!

JEN. Hold on. What's going on, here?

ALYSSA. Oh I just wasn't sure – if in your relationship – you're the – or the –

(*She looks to the other* **WOMEN**.)

Someone help me out, here.

CLEO. The boy or the girl?

ALYSSA. To put it baldly, yes. So I wanted to give you options. I'm sorry. I'm an idiot.

JEN. Why does one of us have to be a man? Couldn't we both just be women?

CLEO. ...No.

RHONDA. Who would take out the trash?

JEN. Both of us! We *both* take out the trash! Okay, I take out the trash. But we're both just people, who happen to be women, who share a house and a bed together. It's really as simple as that. I don't know how to be any more clear with you.

CLEO. ...But you're the boy, right?

ALYSSA. We're *all* kind of being the boy, okay? We're here trying to fix our men like they're microwaves.

JEN. That's not a "man" thing to do, that's a HUMAN thing to do!

And I'm not trying to "fix" her, I just am accustomed to a certain level of peace and calm in my house and when I come home from work I don't think it's too much to ask for her to be happy to see me, for there to be dinner on the table OH MY GOD I'M MY DAD.

MYRA. We all turn into our fathers.

CLEO. Or marry them.

RHONDA. Now THAT'S the patriarchy, right there.

JEN. *(Realizing.)* I'm exactly like my Dad.

This is why I have no real friends.

MYRA. What're you talking about? You're a hoot!

JEN. ...I am?

RHONDA.	**CLEO**.
You're hilarious!	SO fun.

(**JEN** *is moved by this.*)

JEN. Thank you.

ALYSSA. You're perfect. And you deserve Hannah's attention. *(Resetting.)* We can't let them win.

(**ALYSSA** *holds up her body stocking, triumphantly.*)

This is how we can make them forget The Game. This is going to work.

They want us!

We're WOMEN! We're SEXY!

ALYSSA. We're RESOURCEFUL, We're STRONG –

(The baby fusses.)

Okay. Okay.

(The rest of the **WOMEN** *start to get amped.)*

RHONDA. We live longer! And look better!

CLEO. We can grow feet in our stomachs!

JEN. We can manage multiple thoughts AND emotions at one time!

MYRA. AND put a chicken in the crockpot!

ALYSSA. HELL YES!

WOMEN OF TROY, WE ARE WHAT'S REAL! And we are going to make human love to them with our human bodies! Because that's what The Game doesn't have! FLESH! ALEXA! PLAY COUNTRY GIRL POWER POP ANTHEMS!*

(She takes the baby out of the carrier, cradles him in her arms.)

(Back on track:)

We will NOT be NPCs / in our own lives!

MYRA. *(Excited she remembers.)* NON PLAYING CHARACTERS!

ALYSSA. YES MYRA! Because WE are the human women! WE WIN!

THE HUMANS WIN!!!!!

(Excitedly, she tosses the baby up into the air!)

(Everyone shrieks in horror!)

*(**CLEO** catches it!)*

RHONDA.	**JEN.**	**CLEO.**
OH MY GOD!!	WHAT THE HELL	NOOOOO!

ALYSSA. Oh! Sorry! It's not a real baby. I didn't say? / NOT A REAL BABY.

---

*A license to produce *The Game* does not include a performance license for any third-party or copyrighted music. Licensees should create an original composition or use music in the public domain. For further information, please see the Music and Third-Party Materials Use Note on page iii.

CLEO. *(Heart racing.)*   **JEN.**
 NO. YOU DIDN'T.   JESUS!

ALYSSA.   **RHONDA.**
 It's a practice baby!   Oh my *God.*

MYRA. A what?!

ALYSSA. *(Like this is normal.)* A practice baby.

RHONDA. WHAT IN THE HELL.

ALYSSA. I heard about it on a podcast –

The Company's called – Mother? Mother, with a question mark. They're specifically designed for working women who don't have time to decide if they want to have kids.

RHONDA. *(Still horrified, but curious.)* Which podcast?

ALYSSA. One of them! I'm trying to decide, if we want to be parents. But I've been so distracted by work and and all this stuff with Homer I forgot I was holding him which is pretty indicative of my shortcomings as a Mother.

Oh my God. Is my marriage over?

No. It can't be.

    (She holds up her body stocking once again.)

This has to work.

If this doesn't work, then what am I?

    (She goes.)

    (**CLEO,** *this whole time, has been lost deep in her own thoughts.)*

CLEO. Wait. Can we do that?

MYRA. Do what, sweetheart?

CLEO. Are we allowed to – not want kids?

MYRA. *…Yes!*

JEN. You can always say no.

CLEO. *(A real question.)* Can I?

> *(They all sit together, pondering this vast and terrifying question.)*

An Interview

(**HOMER** *is about to be interviewed on Zoom.*)

(He wears a nice collared shirt.)

(Below that, his boxers, which his potential employer can't see.)

(He's sitting at attention. He wants this. His hope shows.)

(He psychs himself up. Starts the Zoom.)

HOMER. Hey, how are ya! No, thank YOU!

Yeah, Margaret's said great things.

I was – class of '07.

Yeah, you have to, these days.

Especially with that kind of infrastructure, yeah.

Yes! I was in management, but I could, ah – I mean, I'm willing to take a step down, I'm a humble guy, he said, humbly.

(She asks a question that makes him uncomfortable.)

Uh, yeah, we can talk about that. Let's get in there! Technically yes, I did quit. But the truth is, they pushed me out. They kept piling more and more projects on me, repeatedly denied my requests for a raise, and when I flagged this in my performance review, they gaslit me, to the point where I thought I was crazy, then they promoted someone beneath me to the position I was basically promised.

It's apparently all the rage right now, it's called "quiet firing" and it's basically the most emasculating way to be terminated because they won't even say it to your fucking face. I started having full-on panic attacks at the office, and then I quit! Technically.

> *(Suddenly, **ALYSSA** enters wearing a full-body lace stocking and not much else.)*

> *(For just a moment, **ALYSSA** is free, she's seductive, she's twenty-five again, her body exists for him and his for her.)*

> *(Then she sees that he's on Zoom, and she is right in front of the camera.)*

> *(**HOMER** catches a glimpse of her. WTF?!)*

> *(Horrified, **ALYSSA** darts back out of the room.)*

> *(**HOMER** keeps his cool, professional smile. Tries to pretend like his wife didn't just parade herself half naked across the screen.)*

Thanks, yeah!

So when exactly are you thinking –

> *(They're telling him they've got a lot of applicants.)*

I get it. You gotta do your due diligence!

No, yeah, if not, just – keep it on the pile. I'll be here!

> *(He laughs, generously.)*

Great to meet you, too.

> *(He hangs up.)*

> *(Feels the vastness of time and the deeper well of his failure.)*

(**ALYSSA** *comes back in, sheepishly. A robe
over her lingerie.*)

What're you / doing?!

ALYSSA. Sorry, I thought you were just playing The Game!

HOMER. I had an interview.

ALYSSA. It wasn't on the calendar.

HOMER. What're you wearing?

ALYSSA. Oh, it's a – stocking. But for your whole – self.

HOMER. You look nice.

ALYSSA. Thank you.

How was the interview?

HOMER. Good! I don't know. Yeah! Good. You never know
with these things. Maybe I'm the guy? Maybe I'm not.
It's metrics. It's not up to me.

And it's kind of a step down. The job.

ALYSSA. So then why'd you take the interview?

HOMER. Because I feel like you've made it clear that you
want me back out there.

ALYSSA. You would take a job that's beneath you, for me?

HOMER. (*It's whatever.*) Yeah, I mean.

(*She kisses him. Tries to start something.*)

HOMER. (*Between kisses.*) I thought this was off the table.

ALYSSA. Yeah, but then I missed you.

(*She starts to really go for it. Reaching into
his boxers.*)

HOMER. Wait.

I don't really – / want –

ALYSSA. What.

Me?

HOMER. No, I just – I'm not really feeling this – right now –

I just had a shitty interview –

(She tries to kiss his neck.)

What're you doing?

ALYSSA. Changing your mind.

HOMER. *NO.*

(He pushes her away. It's awful. She slides off of him, humiliated.)

ALYSSA. Well, if you're not going to have sex with me, could you at least bring the trash cans in?

(Low blow. The lowest.)

HOMER. Could *you*?

ALYSSA. What?

HOMER. I'm just saying you're physically capable of bringing them in yourself, right? You do everything else.

ALYSSA. *Homer.*

HOMER. Equal rights, baby.

(He turns his attention back to The Game.)

ALYSSA. I need YOU to bring them in.

HOMER. Why.

ALYSSA. Because!

HOMER. What do you want from me?!

*(**ALYSSA** says nothing.)*

WHAT. WHAT DO YOU WANT.

ALYSSA. I WANT YOU TO BE A FUCKING MAN.

> *(This hangs there. It's terrible. For both of them.)*

> *(She instantly wishes she could take it back.)*

I'm sorry. You're a man. I know you're a man.

> *(Quietly,* **HOMER** *rips the Xbox from the wall, wraps its cords up around it, pulls off his headset, and hands it all to* **ALYSSA**.*)*

HOMER. Here you go.

> *(***ALYSSA*** *looks at the sad mess of plastic and wires, now a baby in her arms.)*

> *(***HOMER*** *heads towards the stairs.)*

ALYSSA. Where're you going?

Homer, *wait –*

> *(***HOMER*** *leaves.)*

> *(***ALYSSA*** *is left alone with the game console in her arms.)*

> *(Her phone rings.)*

Hi, Dev.

No, now's a great time.

Wow! *Wow.* Really? That's so great! Yes, I'm in! I'm honored!

> *(She listens. She's getting the greatest news of her life. But all she can think about is* **HOMER**. *Tears come, but she pushes them back.)*

ALYSSA. I'm going to give this two hundred percent.

Can't wait to work with you on this.

I'm so happy.

Talk soon.

(She hangs up.)

(The console is still in her arms.)

Pew Pew Pew

(Back in Alyssa's living room. Another night.)

*(All of the **WOMEN**, except for **ALYSSA**, are gathered. **CLEO**, **MYRA**, and **RHONDA** are posing on the couch. **JEN** is trying to get a picture of them. **RHONDA** is now wearing her gorgeous DVF dress.)*

MYRA. CHEESE!

JEN. Myra – your eyes / are closed!

RHONDA. Are we getting / tagged in this?

CLEO. Should we go by the window? / Closer to the light?

MYRA. How about now? Are they open / now?

RHONDA. Wait, Jen, you need to be in the picture!

JEN. No, I do not.

> *(**ALYSSA** enters, in sweats. Haggard. She looks like she's been through a war. She's carrying and taking bites of an entire giant baguette.)*
>
> *(She's surprised to see them.)*

ALYSSA. What're you all doing here?

CLEO. It's Wednesday.

MYRA. Is that – a baguette?

ALYSSA. Yes. I've just been thinking that I'm the breadwinner. I win the bread. But I don't eat bread. Because I have to both win the bread, *AND* fit into my college pants. And why is that fair?! So I'm eating BREAD.

> *(She takes a giant bite.)*

MYRA. Is everything alright, dear?

ALYSSA. ...Homer didn't come home last night.

RHONDA. He's out of the house! That's good!

ALYSSA. ...I don't know where he is.

MYRA. But we have each other! Let's get a group picture!

  *(***ALYSSA*** doesn't move.)*

ALYSSA. We don't need a picture.

MYRA. I'd like one. For my nightstand.

ALYSSA. I *really* don't / want to do a picture –

RHONDA. We'll come to you.

  (They gather around her.)

JEN.
Cleo, a little to your left –
Yes –
Rhonda, let's have you
switch with Myra –
Alyssa, let's have you
center –

CLEO.
Can someone tell me if this
is my good side?

JEN.
Myra had her eyes closed –

RHONDA.
GROUP PICTUREEE!

MYRA.
CHEEESEEEEE!

RHONDA.
Group PICTURE!

ALYSSA.
Myra, open your eyes.

  *(***MYRA*** opens her eyes in a big, weird way.)*

  *(***JEN*** snaps again. Looks. She's not satisfied.)*

JEN.
No thank you.
Let me just get one more –

RHONDA.
Wait – Jen get in the
picture!
Do a selfie –

JEN. This camera does not do selfies.

ALYSSA. JUST TAKE IT, JEN!

JEN. ...Okay, I'm / just –

ALYSSA. What are you all doing here?!

(Hard.)

WHY ARE YOU HERE.

CLEO. ...We're your friends.

ALYSSA. We are not friends. We were united against a common enemy, but we have lost. Game over. Despite the last one hundred years of progress and washable period underwear and Hillary Clinton, we STILL DON'T HAVE ANY POWER.

CLEO. ...Is there a PowerPoint?

ALYSSA. No! No PowerPoint!

Now if you'll excuse me, I have an early morning, and I have to do thirty minutes of cardio before work because I just ate a loaf of bread.

RHONDA. Cardio doesn't actually burn fat, you actually need to be in a / caloric deficit –

ALYSSA. I KNOW, RHONDA. Great dress, by the way.

RHONDA. *(So touched.)* Thank you.

JEN. We can't just give up.

ALYSSA. Oh, but I do. I'll just live here upstairs, and he'll be downstairs going –

(She mimes a fake gun.)

Pew Pew Pew!

Forever. And that's just what it is, now.

It was really nice to meet you all, thank you for the crockpot recipes, and I'll see you in the metaverse.

ALYSSA. Please just – go.

(**MYRA** *stands, taking up lots of space for
maybe the first time in years.*)

MYRA. *(Pissed.)* You think I don't know anything because
I'm old and I use my Kindle as a bookmark!!!!

Well let me tell *you* something.

At the end of your life, after you've buried your parents
and your husband and all three of the cats, it's your
friends that mean everything.

You need to get your head out of your caboose.

CLEO. She means butthole!

ALYSSA. You don't know me. You don't know my life. Go.
Leave.

(*No one moves. No one knows what to do.*)

GET OUT OF MY HOUSE!

(*Suddenly* **MYRA** *pulls an imaginary gun
from her purse.*)

(*Shoots* **ALYSSA**.)

MYRA. PEW PEW PEW!

(*They look at her. What the hell was that?*)

(**ALYSSA** *finds her own imaginary gun.
Shoots* **MYRA**.)

ALYSSA. PEW PEW PEW!

PEW PEW PEW!

(*She shoots someone else.*)

PEW PEW PEW!

(**CLEO** *holds up a fake gun.*)

CLEO. PEW PEW PEW!

(**RHONDA** *wants in on this, too.*)

RHONDA. PEW PEW PEW!

(**JEN** *suddenly, joins in, holding an imaginary bow and arrow.*)

JEN. THWAP! THWAP! THWAP!

(*Suddenly all the* **WOMEN** *hold imaginary weapons, and they're all shooting each other.*)

(*They Pew Pew Pew and Thwap each other for a long time, too long, some dying over the couch, some on the floor. The snacks go everywhere.*)

(*They Pew Pew Pew all of their pent-up rage and frustration.*)

(*Especially* **ALYSSA**. *The murders restore her. It feels amazing.*)

(*It goes on for a long time.*)

(*It keeps going until finally, it's just* **ALYSSA** *standing, breathing amidst a room of corpses. She's killed them all.*)

(*She screams, releasing months, if not years, of pent up worry and longing and stress.* **ALYSSA** *drops her imaginary gun. Trying to catch her breath.*)

(*Someone starts laughing, and then it's a symphony of laughs, laughs that turn to gasps, they're rolling around on the ground laughing, then they're crying.*)

(*But* **ALYSSA** *is really crying.*)

ALYSSA. I can't – I don't –

(**CLEO** *sees that she's fully breaking down.*)

(*She goes to her. Comforts her.*)

CLEO. You're okay.

(*The rest of the* **WOMEN** *join.*)

RHONDA. We're here.

JEN. Just breathe.

MYRA. We're not going anywhere.

ALYSSA. Thank you.

(**CLEO** *holds* **ALYSSA**. *Comforts her. It makes her feel strong.*)

CLEO. I think – I just became a *woman*.

(*They all "Awww," vocalize their support, laugh a bit.*)

ALYSSA. ...I think I really needed that.

JEN. We ALL needed that.

ALYSSA. ...I want to be a Mom. But I'm scared I'll do it wrong. Or I won't be able to do it all.

CLEO. I think – I just became a woman.

(*They all "Awww," vocalize their support, laugh a bit.*)

ALYSSA. My whole life I've been doing it all and it still doesn't feel like it's enough.

I'm not enough.

JEN. See, you ARE though!

RHONDA. You are enough, and then some!

ALYSSA. So wait, am I too much?

MYRA. Sweetheart. You're the right amount. Stop worrying.

ALYSSA. Thanks for being here.

MYRA. Can I PLEASE put one of you down as my emergency contact?

JEN. You can put me down.

MYRA. Really?

JEN. I mean how big of a commitment is this –

(**MYRA** *pulls* **JEN** *into a hug.*)

MYRA. Thank you.

You're my daughters. You're all my daughters.

(*They embrace each other. They are a pile of women, united and strong.*)

(*After a few moments,* **ALYSSA** *leaves them.*)

A Shelter

(Downstairs, in Homer's space.)

(It's quiet, empty, still.)

*(**ALYSSA** enters. She's got a brand new Xbox in a box.)*

(She opens it, she's confused by it. She opens and squints at the directions, and following them, she's able to hook it back up to the TV.)

(The Game's welcome screen glows on her face.)

(Damnit, she's curious. Tired of fighting.)

(She puts the headset on.)

(Reaches for the controller.)

ALYSSA.   Play. Play. How do I just *play*?

(She presses a button, and suddenly, gorgeous sound and light surrounds us. We are transported into The Game, it's breathtakingly real but also magical, there's dew drops and quivering violins and humanity and courage and birds, purple and green and blue.)

(For the first time, it presents itself to us as a full and beautiful and rich world, one that someone like Homer might choose over this one.)

(For the first time, we get it.)

*(And **ALYSSA**. **ALYSSA** gets it. It brings tears to her eyes.)*

ALYSSA. *...Oh.*

> *(She sinks into Homer's chair, works the controller, starts to explore his world.)*
>
> *(Hours pass.)*
>
> *(She plays The Game. Hyper-focused. She looks just like Homer did at the top of the play.)*
>
> *(Quietly, **HOMER** appears in the doorway.)*
>
> *(He's thrown to find her playing The Game.)*

HOMER. ...Having fun?

> *(She instantly jumps to her feet and tries to pretend like she wasn't playing it at all.)*

ALYSSA. Where've you been?

HOMER. The Radisson by the mall.

ALYSSA. *...Why?*

HOMER. I had points.

And I actually went to get a drink with Marcio.

> *(He sits on the couch near her, cautiously. Not sure where they stand.)*

ALYSSA. Your game friend?

HOMER. Yeah.

> *(Then.)*

It was good to meet up. In real life.

(Admitting.) You were right about that. You usually are. It's very annoying.

(This makes her smile.)

(He looks at the screen.)

HOMER. You're playing The Game.

ALYSSA. Trying to. I can't really figure out how to actually play so I've just been exploring the world.

(Then.)

It's really beautiful, Homer.

HOMER. Can I show you my favorite part?

(He holds his hand out to her, she hands him The Game controller.)

*(Moves **ALYSSA**'s player through The Game.)*

ALYSSA. I thought your favorite part was the shooting part?

HOMER. That part gets old. Mostly I like to build stuff.

Here it is.

My Shelter. See?

*(**ALYSSA** leans in, looking at it.)*

See, it's got a bedroom, and a kitchen, and a living room –

And down there, those stairs go down to a cellar where we can store food.

I know, it's not like the stuff *you* build, but.

It's got re-enforced walls for when the storms get bad.

And it's cooler underground. Up to fifteen degrees cooler.

It's what Egyptians used to do, to survive in intense heat. They went underground. So this space is optimal for the Summers.

We could survive anything down here.

ALYSSA. What's the little room right there?

HOMER. Oh, ah.

(He's embarrassed.)

That's for the baby. If you – if we end up doing that.

(Tears come, and he avoids them.)

*(**ALYSSA** studies her husband.)*

ALYSSA. ...You built this for us?

HOMER. Yeah. The other guys, we ah. We look at each other's houses sometimes? We give each other tours. Show each other what we built. We say hey, nice shelter. It can mean something.

(Then.)

I know it's not real.

ALYSSA. ...Yes, it is.

HOMER. I can stop. If you really want me to, I'll stop. I'll throw it away.

(Then.)

Wait no, I'll sell it. That makes more sense.

ALYSSA. No, no.

But I do need you to just – try a little harder. To be with me, here. In *this* world.

HOMER. *(Becoming emotional.)* ...I don't like it here, sometimes.

ALYSSA. I know. And that's okay. But *I'm* here.

(He reaches for her hand. Takes it.)

(Then.) Wanna show me how to play?

HOMER. Really?

ALYSSA. Yeah.

Is there another – / controller thingie?

(Before she can even finish her sentence **HOMER** *finds and produces another controller, like he's been waiting his entire life for her to ask to play with him!)*

(Excited, he hooks it up. Hands her a controller.)

HOMER. You ready for this?

ALYSSA. Yeah!

(They play together.)

(The Game creates a rich, living world around them.)

(A world that's fully real for the both of them.)

(We find them a few hours later, playing The Game.)

(They're now both wearing beauty sheet masks while they play.)

HOMER. Right there – grab that bathtub and drag it over, we can use that if the river floods.

ALYSSA. On it.

Okay – got the tub – but it's full of spiders?

HOMER. Wait no no no gogogogogogo

ALYSSA. AHHHHH

HOMER. SPIDERS ARE BAD

(Of mask.) Is this supposed to sting?

ALYSSA. That means it's working.

(Then.)

WHAT DO I DO?

HOMER. CONTROL B CONTROL B

ALYSSA. THIS IS SO STRESSFUL!

HOMER. I KNOW!

ALYSSA. I HATE THIS GAME

HOMER. KEEP GOING

ALYSSA. Okay – okay – spiders are gone.

HOMER. You crushed that! Here!

(His character tries to do something to her.)

ALYSSA. What is that? What are you doing? Are you slapping me?

HOMER. I'm high-fiving you!

ALYSSA. Oh! Well, I'll – high-five you back.

(She presses buttons on the controller.)

HOMER. Okay, now, *that* was you slapping me.

(They laugh.)

ALYSSA. ...Can we kiss? In The Game?

HOMER. Don't think so.

(Then.)

But in real life, we can.

ALYSSA. Yeah?

(They both slide off their face masks. Look at each other, faces close, both feel incredibly vulnerable and hopeful and scared, like they're about to kiss for the very first time.)

(**HOMER** *takes her chin, and leads her lips to hers. Kisses her softly.*)

(*They smile at each other, a balance restored.*)

(*Again,* **ALYSSA** *addresses us.*)

ALYSSA. I present this image of myself. Playing The Game. Yes, I am to scale.

(*With a game voice.*) THE YEAR IS [insert year]! A group of women band together in a Living Room to fight misogyny and technology and passive aggression! Together, and only together, *they must end the war.*

And, well, they lose! They don't actually end the war, but they do – learn things?

What did I learn? Anything?

I still don't like Games.

(*She thinks.*)

What's that saying? Heaven is other people.

(*She looks back at the* **WOMEN**, *who have formed behind her.*)

And I'll always need them.

Real human people. Saying the wrong thing. Saying the right things. Breathing in my living room. Spilling on my carpet.

(*She goes back to* **HOMER**.)

Carrying me through this world.

HOMER. Who're you talking to?

ALYSSA. ...I have no idea.

(*She returns to her husband, to The Game.*)